*This book
belongs to*

_____

_____

The
Elegant
Elf

AND OTHER ELF AND GOBLIN STORIES

The Elegant Elf

AND OTHER ELF AND GOBLIN STORIES

PARRAGON

First published in Great Britain in 1998 by
Parragon
13 Whiteladies Road
Clifton
Bristol BS8 1PB

ISBN 0 75252-531-X

Printed in Great Britain

Produced by Nicola Baxter
PO Box 71
Diss Norfolk IP22 2DT

Stories by Nicola Baxter
Designed by Amanda Hawkes
Text illustrations by Duncan Gutteridge
Cover illustration by Alisa Tingley

Contents

The
Elegant Elf

Once upon a time, there was an elf who cared for nothing but clothes. Only the finest were good enough for him. If everyone else had five buttons on their jackets, he had six – and they were gold ones, of course. When cloaks were in fashion, the elegant elf's cloak was so long that there was hardly room for it in his cottage.

In fact, most of the rooms in his home were filled with clothes, but the elegant elf didn't mind that. He wanted to keep an eye on his precious jackets and waistcoats, not to mention his socks and knickerbockers!

The elegant elf was sure that nobody could take as much care with his clothes as he liked, so he washed and ironed them himself, paying careful attention to every velvet ruffle and every silken pleat.

It was not surprising that the elegant elf had very little time for anything other than his clothes. In the morning, it took him at least an hour to decide what to wear. First he would look out of the window to see what the weather was like. On a rainy day, he would never go outside, in case his silk stockings got splashed. On a snowy day, he liked to show off his coat made of thistledown, with its wool lining, but he was worried about his hat getting damp, so he only went out when the snow was sparkling underfoot, not falling from the sky. On a sunny day, the elf had an even bigger problem. He liked to wear as many clothes as possible, so that all the other elves could admire them, but that meant he was terribly hot!

Even when he had decided which clothes to wear, it took the elf another hour to get dressed. After all, it takes time to do up one hundred and seventy-two tiny buttons on a satin waistcoat!

The moment of the day that the elf liked best was when he stood in front of the mirror, just before he set off for his walk through the village. His clothes were perfect. Not a speck of dust or a smear of mud could be seen. The elegant elf would sigh with happiness as he admired himself.

Strangely enough, the elf did not know what the other elves thought as they saw him walk slowly down the street. He was sure that they were all admiring him, wishing they had clothes like his, but he never turned his head to make sure, in case it made his hat tip to one side!

In fact, the other elves thought he was very, very silly.

"Did you see him today?" asked Twinkletoes in the bakery one morning. "He was wearing purple boots with gold tassels. Imagine!"

"That's nothing," said Acorn. "Yesterday he had a hat shaped like a dandelion. It looked ridiculous."

"I've never talked to him," said Mayflower, "but I've heard that he's a very stuck-up kind of elf. He thinks he's better than the rest of us."

"I don't think any of us have ever talked to him," agreed

Twinkletoes, "but I'm sure it's true that he's not a very nice elf. It's just as well that he keeps himself to himself."

And that was the way things stayed. No one spoke to the elegant elf and he spoke to no one. The other elves believed that he thought himself too good for them, while he was sure that they all admired him so much that they were afraid to speak to him.

Things might have stayed like that for a very long time – perhaps for ever – if it hadn't been for the Great Storm of Elftown. It happened one autumn day, when the last brown leaves

were swirling from the trees.
First a little breeze began to
blow, and elves going about their
business turned their collars up.
Then dark clouds began to
gather overhead, and elves with
washing drying outside hurried
out to take it in.

Gradually, the wind grew
fiercer. No one was too worried
when old Farmer Fern's fence
blew down, because it always
had been rather rickety. But
when his hen house came flying
down the high street, elves locked
their windows and doors and
huddled closer to the fire. They
had never seen such a storm.

The wind blew and blew, and just when everyone thought that nothing worse could happen, the rain began. It didn't fall in drops. It fell in sheets, as though someone up in the sky was emptying a whole bathtub over Elftown. All the elves who were crouching in their warm houses felt very glad to be indoors, even if a few drops were coming through the roof. They peered out of their windows at the wild weather and hoped that their gardens would not be completely washed away.

The elegant elf, too, was looking out of his window. He

wasn't too worried about the storm but he was worried about how he would get his washing dry. It was sitting in a basket in the kitchen, and he felt sure that his silk knickerbockers would be terribly creased if they were left much longer.

But as the elegant elf gazed anxiously at the sky, he noticed a movement in the street. There in the wind and weather, an elf mother and her little boy were struggling along. Their clothes were wet and cold, and at every second it seemed that the gale would blow them away. They had been in the woods, gathering berries, when the storm began, and were trying desperately to reach their home.

The other elves saw them too, from their cosy homes.

"I wish I could help them," said Mayflower, "but the weather is just too bad."

"Those poor elves," said Twinkletoes sadly. "I'd love to rescue them, but there's no point in three of us being washed away and never seen again."

"They shouldn't have been out so far from home on a day like this," said Acorn. "Some elves don't have the sense they were born with."

The elegant elf didn't say any of those things. He didn't shake his head, or turn his back, or settle down by his fire. He opened his front door and rushed out into the rain, calling out to the half-drowned elves.

Now the elegant elf didn't think for one minute about the golden fringe on his coat or the velvet decorations on his hat, although all of them were ruined in ten seconds flat. He simply ran towards the mother and child, scooped them up under his coat, and carried them back to his cottage, struggling against the wind and rain at every step.

"Well!" cried Twinkletoes, who had seen everything. "Who would have guessed it?"

"I wouldn't have believed it," cried Mayflower, "if I hadn't seen it with my own eyes."

Even Acorn cleared his throat and muttered, "Ahem ... perhaps I've misjudged that elf. He must be good hearted after all."

If you spend a morning in Elftown today, you could almost believe that nothing has changed. The elegant elf still spends all his time thinking about his clothes. He still takes two hours to get ready in the morning. The other elves still don't talk to him or invite him to their houses. But when he walks down the village street each morning, showing off his clothes, every single elf on the street puts down his shopping and, with a loud cheer, claps his hands and stamps his feet. Sometimes the applause can be heard all the way to Goblinville.

Well, the town elves are happy because they feel that they have let him know how they feel about his brave rescue. And the elegant elf is happier still, because he is sure that those elves have seen the error of their ways at last and are finally cheering ... his clothes.

Mayflower's Carrots

Mayflower was a very busy little elf. He had lots of hobbies and was always taking up new ones. As a result, his spare bedroom was full of half-finished projects. There was a model aeroplane with one wing, a cane chair with half a seat, a tapestry with one corner finished, and a pile of newspapers with a heavy weight on top. Between the newspapers were the pressed flowers that Mayflower had collected with great enthusiasm one summer, but Mayflower's wife had forgotten about that and regularly used the papers for lighting the fire.

One afternoon, Mayflower went to visit his old friend Acorn. As he sat in front of the fire, sipping a cup of dandelion tea, the curious elf was surprised to see some brightly coloured rosettes in pride of place above the older elf's fireplace.

"What are those, Acorn?" asked Mayflower, getting up to take a closer look.

"Aha!" smiled Acorn proudly. "Those are my rosettes for winning prizes at last year's Grand Fruit and Vegetable Show in Goblinville. They hold one every summer, you know, but I had never entered until last year."

"And yet you won so many prizes," said Mayflower in surprise. "What about the goblins? Didn't they win anything?"

"I'm afraid those goblins don't know much about gardening," said Acorn. "Oh, they can grow a good toadstool, I'm not denying it, but when it comes to parsnips and beans and potatoes, they don't have a clue!"

Mayflower was very thoughtful as he made his way home that day. He had never had much success with gardening in the past. There had been those extra special daisies that he had sent away for. Every one of them shrivelled and died within weeks. It may partly have been due to the fact that Mayflower almost always forgot to water them, of course.

Then there had been his doomed attempt to grow cacti.

"You can't go wrong, old chap," Twinkletoes had told him. "They need hardly any water at all."

So Mayflower had bought ten different kinds of cactus, each one more prickly than the one before. He was very careful not to water them too little or too much, but month after month passed and still they did not flower.

"It might take years," said Twinkletoes, when Mayflower

complained. "Are you giving them enough sunlight?"

In fact, the cacti were in rather a dark corner, so Mayflower brought them out on to the windowsill, where the sun could reach them. Unfortunately, it was winter, and the sun only peeped out from behind the clouds for a few minutes every day.

"These poor cacti are freezing to death," said Mayflower to his wife. "No wonder they're not flowering." A sensible elf would have waited until spring to see what would happen, but Mayflower, as always, was impatient. He took the cacti and popped them in the oven for a few minutes.

I'm sure I don't need to tell you what happened. Mayflower turned away for a few seconds to make himself a cup of tea. Then he searched for some biscuits in the cupboards. Then he knocked his tea over by mistake and had to start again. By the time the silly elf turned back to rescue his cacti, they were well and truly cooked.

Mayflower vowed that he would never have anything to do with gardening again.

But now Acorn's prizes had set him thinking. Some rosettes above his fireplace would certainly look very fine.

"Now, what did Acorn say he had grown?" Mayflower asked himself. "It was parsnips and beans and potatoes. I must try something else, so that I don't have to compete with Acorn. It will be easy to beat those stupid old goblins."

That night, as he sat down to supper, Mayflower asked his wife to tell him what her favourite vegetables were.

"Oh, I love tomatoes," said Cowslip, "and I'm very fond of carrots too. But why are you asking, Mayflower?"

"Oh, no reason," replied Mayflower airily.

Cowslip gave her husband a suspicious look. She knew that his ideas usually ended in disaster and she was afraid that this would be another one.

"I simply thought that I would try my hand at vegetable growing," her husband explained. It seemed wiser not to mention the Grand Fruit and Vegetable Show yet, just

in case the vegetables were not a
great success.

Cowslip thought for a moment.
She really couldn't see how things
could go badly wrong, and it
would be nice to have some really
fresh vegetables for a change.

Over the next few weeks,
Mayflower worked very hard. No
one could say that the elf was not
making every effort to do things
the right way. He found a book in
the Elf and Goblin Visiting Library
about vegetable growing and read
everything it said on Preparing the
Soil. For a whole week he dug and
forked and raked in the back
garden, until he had a little plot

that looked as trim and neat as the one he had glimpsed through Acorn's window. Then he set off to Goblinville to buy his seed.

The shops in Goblinville are much bigger than those in Elftown. Mayflower visited several before he found that the ironmonger's also sold vegetable seed. But what a lot of different packets there were to choose from! And they all had such pretty pictures on the front.

Mayflower looked at the carrot packets first. Sweet and Small, Tasty and Tiny, and Mini Mouthful were good names for carrots, but they didn't sound quite right for a vegetable show. Mayflower had a feeling that vegetables needed to be big if they were to win prizes.

The eager elf was just beginning to feel discouraged when he spotted a slightly larger packet at the back of the rack. It looked rather old and dusty, but the name in big, old-fashioned letters on the front made Mayflower very happy.

"GOBLIN'S ORANGE GIANT," he read, "that's the one for me, no doubt about it."

Mayflower was so pleased with his discovery that he forgot all about the tomatoes. He hurried home with his packet and sat down to read the instructions.

Now it may be that you don't know very much about goblin gardening, and Mayflower was just the same. Acorn was wrong when he said that goblins could not grow fine vegetables. In fact, goblins can grow anything they want to, because they use magic. As magic is not allowed in the Grand Fruit and Vegetable Show, very few goblins bother to use non-magical methods and enter the show.

Some elves are very good at magic, too, but it may not surprise you to learn that Mayflower had never managed to pass his First Proficiency Badge at school. And evening classes since then hadn't helped very much either.

That is why, when Mayflower read the instructions on the packet, he didn't realize that magic was involved. He thought that everyone recited a few words over their carrot seed once it was in the ground. If he had known that it was magic, I think that even Mayflower would not have been silly enough to try it. But on the other hand...

So, on the day following a new moon, as the packet advised, Mayflower stood in his garden, looking down at one neat row of carrot seed and said:

Hobble gobble, wind blow,
Rain fall and carrots grow.
Hobble gobble, sun shine,
Dig them up and they'll be fine.

I must warn you now, if you ever decide to grow carrots, don't *ever* say that rhyme within their hearing. The results could be too disastrous to think about.

Poor Mayflower! Perhaps it was a pity that the weather just then decided to be very changeable. That night, the wind blew and the rain came down. In the morning, the sun shone over the whole of Elftown … but not into Mayflower's bedroom, which was as dark as if it were the middle of the night.

I expect you can guess what had happened. Overnight, the whole row of carrots had grown … and grown … and GROWN! Their tops were covering Mayflower's bedroom window, so that not a twinkle of sunshine could peep through. And the orange roots of the carrots, appearing through the soil, were so big that they filled the whole garden.

If it had been left to Mayflower, it might have been ages before the problem was discovered. He just kept opening his eyes and saying, "Oh, it's still night. I can have another little sleep." This might have gone on all day, but Cowslip knew at once that something was wrong. Apart from anything else, there was a strong smell of *carrot* all through the house!

"I'll get to the bottom of this," she said, and she stormed out of the front door in her dressing gown. When she saw the giant carrots, poor Cowslip sat down and laughed until the tears ran down her face. It wasn't really funny to have a garden full of giant carrots, but somehow she couldn't help herself.

"Come out here, Mayflower!" she called. "Look at your gardening. It's been … well … rather too successful!"

For one brief moment, Mayflower's spirits soared when he saw the giant carrots.

"They will win a prize for sure," he cried happily. "Poor old Acorn can't beat this!"

"What prize?" asked Cowslip. "And what's it got to do with Acorn? Now, Mayflower, tell me everything."

And that's what Mayflower did.

"You are a noodle, Mayflower," said Cowslip. "You can't win a prize with these carrots. How on earth do you think you are going to dig them up?"

Mayflower's face fell. "Perhaps if I asked some friends to help…" he began hopefully.

"And how do you think you are going to take them to Goblinville?" asked Cowslip.

"Oh … er … well…" Mayflower could not think of anything to say at all. "What are we going to do?" he asked in a small voice, after a long silence.

"There is only one thing we can do," said Cowslip firmly. "We must go and ask my uncle the goblin for help. I don't like doing it, because he doesn't have a very high opinion of elves anyway, but in this situation, we have no other choice, I'm afraid."

So this time it was Cowslip who set off for Goblinville, having given Mayflower strict instructions about several important jobs that needed doing inside the house.

Cowslip spent a long time with her uncle. He laughed so hard when he heard the story that he could hardly speak for an hour or so. When at last he could talk without giggling, he wrote down a few important words for his niece on a piece of paper.

That evening, Cowslip and Mayflower stood in a tiny corner of the garden as the carrots towered over them. Cowslip read from her piece of paper:

Hobble gobble, wind blow,
Rain fall and carrots go.
Hobble gobble, sun shine,
Go to bed and you'll be fine.

When he woke in the morning, Mayflower hardly dared to open his eyes. But when he did so, he saw golden sunshine pouring into the bedroom. Down in the garden, there was not a carrot to be seen, just some rather large holes and a slightly startled rabbit.

Mayflower began to feel very much better. When he thought about it, his gardening had been quite a success. The only trouble was that it had been *too much* of a success. Perhaps if he didn't try quite so hard next time…

Cowslip came down to breakfast to find her husband pulling on his boots, his travelling hat by his side. She gave him one very serious look.

"I thought I'd go into Goblinville," said Mayflower, "to buy some tomato seed. You said how much you liked tomatoes. This time I'd make sure I didn't…"

Mayflower's voice trailed off as he saw the expression on Cowslip's face.

"Or…" he said quickly, "I might just go in and buy some tomatoes instead. How would that be?"

"That would be much, much better," said Cowslip. And it was.

The Elf
in the
Tree

Once there was an elf who really hated housework. He hated tidying up and dusting and sweeping and polishing. Most of all, he hated washing up. All those bubbles got up his rather long nose and made him sneeze. And the water made his cuffs soggy.

"Why don't you do it all just once a week?" suggested one friend. "Then it would be over and done with for another thirteen days." (Elf weeks are not quite the same as ours, but it would take too long to explain why. Months are different too, but they don't come into this story, so it doesn't matter. And as for elf clocks…)

Well, Hollyhock (for that was his name) thought that the once-a-week idea was an excellent one. The only trouble was that he never could decide which day would be the best to begin. Each morning when he woke up he thought, "Oh no, I couldn't face it today." So the dust kept settling and the dishes kept piling up in the sink.

What with one thing and another, the house began to be rather *smelly*. Hollyhock grew so used to it that he didn't really mind very much, but he did notice that most of his friends had stopped coming to see him, and he wondered why.

"Er, Tumbledown," he said one day. "Is there … is there … anything I should know about? I mean elves used to be dropping in every day, but now I hardly see anyone from one week to the next."

Now it was well known that Tumbledown had no sense of smell at all, ever since he had put his head into a pepper mine and sneezed so hard that his ears almost fell off. But there was nothing wrong with Tumbledown's ears now, and he had heard the other elves complaining about Hollyhock's house. Still, it was a delicate matter, and he didn't quite know how to begin.

"I believe, my old friend, that it's a matter of ... well ... *odour*," he said hesitantly.

"What?" asked Hollyhock. "What's *odour*?"

"It's ... well ... it's a certain lack of ... er ... *fragrance*," stuttered Tumbledown, his face growing red.

"I still don't understand what you're talking about," replied his friend. "What is it that my house doesn't have?"

"To put it plainly," replied Tumbledown, "your house doesn't have a pleasant *aroma*."

Hollyhook looked blank. "I still haven't got the faintest idea what you mean," he said. "Please tell me in simple words, Tumbledown. If you won't tell me the truth, who can I ask?"

Then Tumbledown took pity on his friend. Putting an arm across the young elf's shoulder, he said kindly, "My boy, your house *smells*. That's why no one comes to visit you any more. It doesn't worry me, since my visit to the pepper mine, but it upsets the other elves a good deal."

Hollyhook went very pink and looked around him. The house was in a terrible state. Cobwebs hung across the windows and dust lay thick on the table. There was a half-eaten sandwich on the chair and a mouldy apple on the shelf. And yes, even he had to admit it, there was a strange and not very pleasant smell about the place.

Tumbledown looked at his friend and felt sure that the young elf would now take steps to clean up the house. But Hollyhock's next words were the last ones he expected to hear.

"In that case," said Hollyhock, "I'll leave the house and go to live in a tree."

Tumbledown rubbed his ears. Maybe that sneezing in the pepper mine *had* permanently affected them. But Hollyhock was speaking again, and even more firmly.

"Yes," he said, "that's exactly what I'll do. There's no nonsense about housework if you live in a tree, and everything smells nice *all* the time."

"But the cold … and the wind … and the rain!" cried Tumbledown, who liked to be comfortable.

"I shall make myself a little house," explained Hollyhock, "just big enough to keep me warm and dry, but *not* big enough to need furniture. And when it needs cleaning and dusting, I shall open the doors and windows and let the wind and the rain do the job for me. I don't know why I didn't think of it before. In fact, I don't know why *all* elves don't live in trees. I'm sure I've read that they used to in the old days."

Tumbledown had to admit that he had heard something similar himself, so perhaps it wasn't such a crazy idea after all.

"I'll come with you and help you to choose a suitable tree," he said. "That will be very important."

Several elves wondered why Hollyhock and Tumbledown were spending so much time walking up and down in Shady Wood. They were even more surprised when the two elves began to carry planks of wood into the trees.

"What on earth can he be doing?" asked Cowslip, as she finished her shopping one morning and almost bumped into Hollyhock, tottering along under the weight of a large mattress. "I thought my Mayflower was the silliest elf in town, but now I'm not so sure."

The very next day, her question was answered, when every elf in the town received an invitation.

This is what it said:

HOLLYHOCK ELF

invites you to his

TREEHOUSE WARMING

(four trees from the holly bush in Shady Wood)

PLEASE BRING A BOTTLE

OF SOMETHING NICE.

Well, there wasn't an elf in Elftown who wasn't eager to see exactly what had been happening in Shady Wood, especially when another notice appeared on Hollyhock's cottage, pinned to the middle of the front door.

Gone to live in Shady Wood.

No deliveries here please.

All the elves trooped into the wood, looking all around for signs of a little house among the trees. But at the foot of the fourth tree from the holly bush, they could see nothing at all.

"Yoohoo!" called a voice. "I'm up here, neighbours!"

And there was Hollyhock, peering out of a tiny little house, high up in the branches of the tree.

Cowslip asked what everyone was thinking. "But why?" she called. "What was wrong with your nice little house in town?"

"Let's just say," said Hollyhock, "that it had certain disadvantages. I don't want to say anything else about it. This cosy treehouse is much more my style."

Elves are good at giving parties, and the one that followed was remembered for a very long time. By the time the last elf wandered home, Hollyhock's new home was well and truly warmed.

That night, Hollyhock tucked himself up in his new bed and felt happier than he had been for a long time. He closed his eyes and drifted off to sleep to the sound of rustling leaves and the sighing of the wind.

Hollyhock was very tired that night, and he slept well. The next day, lots of his old friends came back to visit him. It was just like the old days, and Hollyhock enjoyed chatting and laughing with the other elves even more for being on his own so long.

But that night, the peaceful world of the treetops changed. The wind rose and, instead of sighing through the branches, it howled. Even the large branches, on which the treehouse was perched, began to sway. Hollyhock woke in the middle of the night feeling not seasick but treesick.

Then there were the little woodland noises that sound so pleasant during the day and so very worrying at night – little squeaks and squeals, some growls, and some snorting and snuffling.

By the morning, Hollyhock was a nervous wreck.

"*Anything* is better than this," he said to himself, climbing unsteadily down the tree. "There is only one thing to do."

And that is why the elves who passed his town house that day heard a lot of huffing and puffing inside and saw a new notice on the front door.

SPRING CLEANING
in progress.
Please visit tomorrow
(and every day after that!)

Sleepy
Snowdrop

You may have met many elves in your time, but I'm sure that you've never met one that was as sleepy as Snowdrop.

Everyone in Elftown knew that it was quite usual to come across Snowdrop lying peacefully asleep almost anywhere.

Cowslip once fell over her, sleeping in the sun outside the bakery. Twinkletoes sprayed her with water once when he was washing his wheelbarrow. She had crept inside and fallen fast asleep. It all became more than a joke when old Mrs Mallow nearly collapsed with fright when she opened her shed and saw a little face peering back at her. After all, no one expects to find a sleeping elf in her potting shed!

Some of the elves got together to decide what to do.

"I say that little elf is just lazy," grumbled Acorn. "You never heard of elves falling asleep during the day when *I* was young, I can tell you. It's a disgrace and must be stopped."

"Perhaps she's ill," said Cowslip. "Maybe she has a kind of sleeping illness and needs some medicine."

"Nonsense!" cried Acorn. "Old Doctor Driftwood from Goblinville had a look at her only the other week, and he said that she was perfectly fine. You know how wise those goblin doctors are."

"I think she's under a spell," said Mayflower, who had recently had quite a lot of trouble from magic. "Maybe a wicked wizard has enchanted her, so that she can hardly keep her eyes open."

Everyone was a little quiet after this. It certainly was something to think about. But on the whole, it seemed unlikely.

"There hasn't been a wizard through here for at least a couple of years," said Acorn, "and come to think of it, Snowdrop was a perfectly ordinary little elf then.

I still say she's lazy. Young elves today don't know what hard work is. When I was young…"

"Yes, yes," Cowslip broke in. Once he got started, Acorn could keep on all day about what happened when he was a boy. "The question is," Cowslip went on quickly, "what are we going to do? Things can't go on like this. Someone – probably Snowdrop herself – is going to get hurt."

"I think we should go and talk to her mother," suggested Twinkletoes. "She should really sort this out."

"But didn't you know?" asked Mayflower. "Her mother has been rather poorly for a long time now. I don't think we should worry her. We should try to solve the problem by ourselves."

"Someone should follow Snowdrop," said Acorn, "and see where she goes. Then at least we can stop her falling asleep somewhere dangerous. We can take turns."

So it was agreed. Twinkletoes waited outside Snowdrop's house the first morning until she came out. He followed her to the shops, where she bought some elf bread and a bag of apples. She put them in her basket and turned to visit the greengrocer's. Then, to

Twinkletoes' surprise, she fell asleep right in the middle of the road! Of course, the kindly elf woke her at once, before a goblin carriage ran her over. Then he helped her to pick up her apples, which had rolled all over the street and across the pavement.

After that, it wasn't much use following her further, because she knew perfectly well that poor Twinkletoes was there!

Next day it was Acorn's turn. The old elf couldn't move as quickly as Twinkletoes, but then Snowdrop walked along dragging her feet as well, so it didn't really matter. Acorn followed the sleepy girl out into the countryside, where she began to pick berries. But after only a few minutes, she sank down into a bramble bush and fell fast asleep.

Even Acorn couldn't help but feel sorry for her when he saw her poor scratched hands as he helped her out of the brambles.

On the third day, Mayflower followed Snowdrop down to the river, where she began to pick some flowers. But before very long, she sat down on the sunny bank and closed her eyes.

Luckily, Mayflower stayed watching for a while, because in a few minutes the little elf, still fast asleep, rolled down the bank and fell, with hardly a splash, into the deep, swirling water!

Mayflower may have been rather silly about some things, but he was a very good swimmer. Without a thought, he jumped into the fast-flowing water and swam strongly after the little elf, who had fallen on to a floating lily leaf and had not even woken as she was swept down the river.

Within a few minutes, Mayflower had pulled the dripping elf from the river.

"I'm going to take you home to Cowslip," he said kindly. "She will find us both some dry clothes and know what to do next."

When Cowslip saw the two soaking elves, she hurried them inside. After hot baths and a steaming mug of elf tea, they both felt better. And Cowslip told Mayflower that he had been an extremely brave elf and she was very proud of him indeed.

Then Cowslip turned to Snowdrop with a smile and said softly, "My dear, I think it is time

that you and I went to see your
mother. I think I know what is
happening, and it is high time
that it was sorted out. We will
take this apple pie with us."

So Snowdrop and Cowslip
walked slowly through Elftown,
until they came to the tumbledown
cottage where Snowdrop lived
with her mother.

Inside, everything was neat and
tidy. The furniture was polished
and gleamed in the lamplight.
There were flowers in the vases
and piles of freshly ironed
washing waiting to be put away.
Snowdrop led the way upstairs,
where, in a little bedroom that

was as neat and tidy as any elf's room you have ever seen, a frail lady sat in a comfortable bed.

"How lovely to see you," she said to Cowslip. "I've often asked Snowdrop to bring her friends home, but she is always so busy. The doctor says that I shall be fine as long as I don't overdo it for a while. In the meantime, Snowdrop keeps the house looking beautiful. She cooks me lovely meals and does all the washing and ironing. I don't know how she finds time to do everything she does for me."

"I do," said Cowslip gently. "Little Snowdrop works half the

night to make everything nice for you. Then she falls asleep during the day because she is so tired. We are all very proud of her, but it is time that we made some better arrangement. How about this..." And Cowslip went on to explain what she had in mind.

Snowdrop's mother is better now, and Snowdrop has never again fallen asleep except in her own little bed. That's because every elf in Elftown helped her for a while. And who did the most? Old Acorn felt so badly about his harsh words that he spent all his time doing what he could ... until *he* fell asleep in the cabbage patch!

The Goblin
Gathering

Every so often, there is a great event in the lives of goblins everywhere. That is when the new goblin King is chosen. Then goblins from far and wide come together to make the choice. This event is called the Goblin Gathering, and if you ever get the chance to attend one, I recommend you to do so. It is not like any other gathering in all the fairy lands.

For one thing, goblins enjoy a good argument more than anything else in the world, except perhaps a toadstool stew and a cup of juniper juice, which would make anyone else very ill indeed but somehow seem to suit hardy goblin digestions.

But during a Goblin Gathering, juniper juice and toadstool stew are hardly thought of. The goblins are much more interested in arguing with each other about the good and bad points of all the candidates for the post of King.

In fact, this is such a sight to see that sometimes elves creep up and watch when they think that the goblins are so busy arguing they won't notice a ring of bright little eyes in the background. For elf Kings are born, not chosen.

At the time of this story, the old goblin King had just died, as goblin Kings do when they are very, very old. As you know, goblins live much longer than humans, sometimes as much as three hundred years.

Now a goblin King must be wise and kind. He must listen carefully to what goblins are saying and make sure that the old goblin ways are remembered. For goblins know a great deal that even elves have forgotten, such as how to make snowflakes and where to find the nest of the magic phoenix bird in the middle of the desert.

At this Gathering, there were three candidates for the post of King. The first was Griffin, a tall goblin with a long beard. He was said to have read every goblin book ever written, and that is a very big number indeed.

The second candidate was Borage, who knew more about goblin traditions than any other goblin. He could tell you when goblins first learnt to make thistledown and the names of all the goblin Kings from the beginning of time.

Last but by no means least was Burdock, the kindest goblin you ever met. Some people, especially elves, think that goblins are rather fierce and unfriendly, but Burdock was not like that at all. He went out of his way to be nice to everyone, and if you were in trouble, he was the first goblin you would turn to.

These goblins came to the forest to answer the Three Questions.

All the other goblins gathered round, anxious to hear their answers. By tradition, the oldest goblin of all asked the questions.

The first was a history question. "When," asked the oldest goblin, "did the Great King Tempest build the first goblin town?"

"It was in the third year of his reign," replied Griffin, who had read King Tempest's own book on the subject.

"No," said Borage, "what a foolish thing to say. It was in the fourth year of his reign. King Tempest himself made a mistake when he wrote his own book. Every historian knows that."

Burdock spoke last. "I don't know which of my friends here is correct," he said. "Does it really matter? Surely what we need to worry about is how well we build goblin towns today."

At that, all the goblins began to discuss the answers of the three candidates. Above the noise, a clear voice could be heard. It was Swallow, the daughter of the last King.

"Indeed, it is true that there was a mistake in King Tempest's book," she said, "but it was not he who made it. The scribe who copied out the King's notes found it hard to read his writing and made a small error. It was not his fault, and the fact has been put right in more recent versions of the book. We must always try to be fair about the past. Only then can we act well in the present and the future."

There was a small silence. The goblins had been given plenty to think about. Then the oldest goblin asked the second question.

"If the King's palace caught fire," he said, "and there was only time to save one thing from the flames, would you save a little goblin kitchen boy, hiding under a table, or the great Crown of Crowns with its gold and jewels?"

"That is not an easy question," replied Griffin. "Naturally, one would wish to save the boy, but the Crown of Crowns is unique. It can never be replaced, and it was the Great Wizard who first made it. We have a duty to save as much of our goblin history as we can. Regretfully, I would choose the Crown of Crowns."

"This time my rival is right," said Borage, "although his answer was expressed in such a long-winded way that I almost fell asleep. A King must often make hard choices. I do not shrink from that. The Crown of Crowns is of enormous importance in goblin history. It must be saved."

When Burdock spoke, his voice shook with emotion. "There is no question in my mind," he said. "The life of a single goblin is worth more than any crown. I would save the boy."

Once again, everyone spoke at once, but Swallow's voice again rose above them all.

"My friend Burdock is right," she said. "Every goblin is precious. But our history is important too. A question like this should not arise. If some little singing birds were allowed to fly through the palace night and day, in return for good food and a comfortable nest, they would warn us at the very first sign of a fire. Then it could be put out long before the crown or the boy were in danger."

One again there was a hush after she had spoken, before the oldest goblin asked his final question to the candidates.

"What is the most important thing you can see at this moment?" he asked, turning to look at the three goblins.

This time, it was Borage who spoke first. "The throne," he said simply, "which has been carried here from the royal palace. I hope to be seated upon it before the day is over."

Griffin gave a small smile and took from his robe a mirror of polished silver. Holding it up to his face, he said, "Myself! I am the goblin who will hold the future of all goblins in his hands. A King cannot afford false modesty. I am the most important thing that I can see."

"My friends," cried Burdock. "I am astonished at these answers, although I am sure they are well meant. The most important things that I can see are the faces of every goblin here and the love for our goblin people that I see shining out of them. That is what is truly important, and we should not forget it."

As the candidates finished their answers, the noise was deafening. But one or two goblins waited to hear what Swallow would say. Her calm voice seemed to still the gathering as she began to speak.

"I love our goblin people," she said, "but I see something without which no living thing could survive. Not a goblin, not a bird, not a flower, not a tree. It is the sunlight, sparkling through the branches. That is more important than all our words and deeds."

Now the arguments began in earnest. Each goblin had a favourite among the candidates. Voices rose and the talk was hot and fierce. The elves watching in the background hugged themselves with glee. Who would win this contest and rule the whole of the goblin kingdom?

Above the shouts of the crowd, a voice called for silence. To everyone's surprise, it was the oldest goblin who spoke.

"To my mind," he said solemnly, "one goblin alone has shown wisdom, learning and kindness today. That person should be our next ruler. Goblins, I beg you to greet in the time-honoured fashion, our first and only Queen … Swallow!"

In the space of a heartbeat, every goblin present knew that he was right, and a great cheer rose up among the branches. Another Goblin Gathering had come to its right and proper end.

How Petal Found a Home

It is a tradition among goblins that if another goblin asks for shelter, they should be given it. But sometimes things don't quite work out like that.

There was once a goblin called Petal. She worked as a cook in a large goblin home, where she was treated as one of the family. But gradually, the children left home to find work and homes of their own, and at last there was no more work for Petal to do, and she knew that she would have to leave.

"Don't worry," she told the mother of the family, "at least among goblins you are always sure of a bed for the night if you have no home to go to.

Petal set out to travel to the village where she was born. She knew that there would be goblins who still remembered her, and she hoped to find another home where she could cook and look after the family.

It was a long journey, but Petal found friendly faces wherever she went because she was a friendly goblin herself.

When she reached her own village, however, things were rather different. The first person she saw was old Mr Mumbles, who was digging in his garden.

"Hello, Mr Mumbles," called Petal. "Do you remember me? I used to live here, in the little cottage by the stream."

"You do look familiar, my dear," said Mr Mumbles, "although my eyes are not as good as they used to be. How can I help you?"

"I was hoping," said Petal, "that you would be able to have me to stay with you until I find a place of my own. I'll be no trouble and I can cook for you."

"Oh dear," said Mr Mumbles, "I'm afraid that won't do at all. My sister is staying with us at the moment, so we don't have a spare room. And anyway, I'm afraid my wife might not like another goblin in her kitchen."

"Never mind," said Petal cheerfully, "I'll ask someone else. Good afternoon, Mr Mumbles!"

Petal walked on into the village. It was a lovely, sunny day, and she soon came across Mulberry, hanging out rows and rows of washing.

"Hello, Mulberry! Do you remember me?" asked Petal, giving a friendly smile.

"Of course I do. It's Petal, isn't it?" cried Mulberry. "How lovely to see you again. Are you coming back to live with us?"

"Yes, indeed," said Petal. "And I was wondering if you would be able to have me to stay with you while I'm finding my feet. Would that be all right?"

"Oh, Petal," said Mulberry. "I do wish that I could help you. Since you went away, Mudlark and I have had three little boys, and there isn't an inch of space anywhere in our cottage. I am so sorry. Perhaps you could try Daisy down the road."

"I will," said Petal. "Goodbye!"

Daisy was not at home when Petal knocked on her door, but by chance Petal met her coming down the street with her shopping basket. The two goblins were very happy to see each other. They had grown up together and been in the same class at the goblin school.

"I'm so sorry I was out when you called," said Daisy, "but I had to get some things for supper. My whole house is being redecorated, and I can't use the kitchen at the moment, so I've bought some rolls instead."

"I suppose that means you don't have much room for a

visitor at the moment?" asked Petal, her heart sinking.

"My dear, I'm so sorry," said Daisy, "but you would be sleeping with your feet in a paint pot!"

Petal was beginning to feel that even that would be better than nothing, but she smiled cheerfully and went on her way.

Mrs Gooseberry was coming out of the bakery. "Why, if it isn't Petal!" she called in a friendly way. "What have you been doing with yourself? It must be years since you were back here. I hope you'll be staying this time. I'm afraid I can't stop. I'm rushing home to cook tea for some visitors and I've got just half an hour to do it in."

"But…" Petal began. She need not have bothered. Mrs Gooseberry was already halfway down the street.

Poor Petal was just beginning to think that she would have to lie down under a hedge that night, when she passed an empty shop. It was rather shabby, but Petal could see that it had once been a fine building.

"Do you know who owns this building?" Petal asked a passing goblin, for an idea had come into her mind. "If I can't stay with anybody and cook in their home," she said to herself, "I'll start my own restaurant. Everyone seems to be so busy and in such a hurry, I'm sure they'd like to come and eat out every once in a while. It would be a treat for everyone."

And that is just what happened. That very afternoon, Petal found the owner of the shop and persuaded her to let her move into the building. Then she rolled up her sleeves and set to work. Less than a week later, half the village was coming to eat at Petal's Parlour.

"I don't know what we did without you, my dear," said Mrs Mumbles. "My sister-in-law was always trying to help in the kitchen, and she's a terrible cook. I'm glad to get out and eat some delicious food again."

Everyone was glad that Petal had come back, and you can be sure that any stranger visiting the village will find a bed for the night at Petal's Parlour.

A Bee
in a
Bonnet!

Goblins and elves do not mix a great deal. Goblins tend to think that elves are not very serious and take life rather too lightly, while elves believe that goblins are fierce and argue at every opportunity. Both would admit, however, that there are clever goblins and clever elves. In the case of the bee in a bonnet, both of them were needed.

Old Mother Sedge was an elf who kept bees. Elves are very fond of sweet things, and Old Mother Sedge's elderflower honey was much in demand. So when Old Mother Sedge came running into the bakery one day shouting that her bees had flown away, everyone knew that this was a real emergency.

"Don't worry, Mother Sedge," said Twinkletoes, who was collecting some bread for his neighbour, "we'll all go and look for your bees. We'll soon find them, I promise."

Old other Sedge looked a little doubtful. She knew that it is not an easy matter to find bees. But she smiled and thanked the young elf.

"If you find them, Twinkletoes," she said, "I'll give you an extra large jar of my special honey. And I mean a *large* jar."

Twinkletoes rushed off as fast as his legs would carry him. As he ran, his mind was in a whirl.

"I must try to think like a bee," he said to himself, which was really rather difficult. Who knows how bees think?

"I only know three things about bees," said Mayflower when Twinkletoes asked him for help. "They buzz, they make honey and they *sting*. I don't want an angry bee coming after me, thank you very much. You'd better look for them on your own, my friend."

Twinkletoes hurried off to old Acorn. He knew that he would do best to flatter the old elf.

"Acorn," he said, "I'm sorry to take up your precious time, but I badly need the advice of an older and wiser elf."

Acorn was not deceived. "What do you want, Twinkletoes?" he asked sharply. "If it's about borrowing my top hat again, you can forget it. It's never been the same since you borrowed it last time. Now what is it? I'm in a hurry today."

"It's about bees," said Twinkletoes. "Old Mother Sedge's bees have flown away, and I've promised to help her to get them back."

"There is only one piece of advice I can give you about bees, young elf," said Acorn, "and that is to stay as far away from them as you can. Mother Sedge (and not so much of the old, if you don't mind) has a way with bees. They know when they're dealing with a person who understands them. You, my lad, do not have a way with bees. You are better to leave well alone."

Poor Twinkletoes did not know
what to do. He consulted all his
friends and relations, but no one
knew what to do. Then he went
to the Elf and Goblin Visiting
Library and found a book about
bees. It said, "Bees can be
dangerous. They should only be
approached by an expert and
then only with great care."

It was not encouraging, but
Twinkletoes thought about the
extra large jar of honey he might
have if he could only find those
bees. There was just one more
person he could think of to ask
for advice, but he was not an elf.
He was a goblin.

Goblin Merryweather lived on the outskirts of Goblinville. Some people said that he was a wizard in disguise, but in fact he was just a very wise man who liked to keep himself to himself.

He was sitting outside with a book on a fine summer's evening when Twinkletoes came hurrying along. Merryweather knew the young elf by sight, but they had never spoken, so he was surprised when Twinkletoes came straight up the garden path and politely doffed his cap.

"Can I help you?" asked the goblin. "It's Twinkletoes, isn't it? I don't often see you hereabouts."

"No, sir," replied Twinkletoes, "but I have a great favour to ask you, and I wanted to come as soon as possible."

Then he told Merryweather all about the bees and how he would like to find them for Old Mother Sedge. He even told Merryweather *why* he wanted to find them!

"Well, well," said Merryweather, "you have set yourself a difficult task. Bees are strange creatures. Old Mother Sedge is a wise woman. If she can't catch them, I'm not sure that anyone can."

"I have to try," said his visitor, "I've promised her I will."

"So you have," agreed the wise old goblin, "and I will help you if I can. Now, what have you thought of so far?"

Twinkletoes explained that he had tried to think in the way that bees would think, but he had found it rather difficult."

"It *is* difficult," said Merryweather, "but you are certainly on the right track. You strike me as being quite a clever young elf. Let us put our heads together and see what we can think up."

Merryweather and Twinkletoes stayed talking late into the night. They looked at books, and drew diagrams, and considered all kinds of ways to attract the bees.

"It doesn't matter how silly the idea is," said Merryweather, "there may be the germ of an answer to our problem in it."

"Well, one idea I had," said Twinkletoes, "was to dress up as a bee and see if other bees would come along to say hello."

Merryweather looked at him for a moment. "That, I have to say, *is* a very silly idea," he said. "And quite frankly, I think the sight of you in a bee costume would send any self-respecting bee flying off in the opposite direction straight away. Now, let us think more seriously for a minute. I'm sure there is a better way to go about this."

"The other thing I was thinking," said Twinkletoes slowly, for he did not want to be laughed at again, "was that bees like flowers more than anything else, so if I could find a specially big flower, they might want to come to visit it, especially if it was a flower they hadn't seen before."

"Now there, young elf, I think you do have an idea," said the goblin thoughtfully, "but where can we find a large, unusual flower? I don't know of anywhere around here."

"Neither do I," said the elf
sadly, "but I had better go now.
Thank you so much for your
help, Merryweather." And he
picked up his hat, ready to leave.

Just at that moment, a strange
look came over the old goblin's
face. He leaped out of his chair
and gave Twinkletoes a thump
on the back that sent him flying.

"I've got it!" he cried. "You just
gave me a wonderful idea!"

Merryweather led Twinkletoes
up to his attic. There among the
cobwebs was a large trunk.

"My Great Aunt Amarylis's
things are in here," he said.
"She's been gone for many years
now, but I remember something
of hers that I think will help. Ah!
Here it is!"

And he held up the most
extraordinary bonnet you have
ever seen. It was made of
feathers of every colour of the
rainbow, and they were arranged
round and round a yellow
middle, just like the petals of a
very strange flower.

"That's perfect," said the elf.

Next morning, bright and early,
the goblin and the elf hid in Old
Mother Sedge's orchard. They
had put the hat down on the
grass, where any passing bee
could see it.

It was such warm, sunny
morning, and the two bee-
catchers had had very little
sleep the night before, so
perhaps it was not surprising
that they dozed off under the
apple trees.

They were woken by the loudest buzzing you have ever heard. And it was coming from the famous hat!

If you had visited Twinkletoes that evening, it would have been hard to hold a conversation with him, for his mouth was so full of delicious honey, he could hardly speak. Old Mother Sedge gave her bees a stern talking to, and they have not strayed again – unfortunately for Twinkletoes!

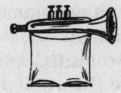

Trouble
in
Elftown

Now you might think that Elftown is a fairly quiet place, and ninety-nine days out of a hundred, you would be right. Once in a while, though, there is *trouble*, and the usual peaceful life of Elftown disappears overnight. That is exactly what happened when Twinkletoes decided to learn the trumpet.

Trumpets can be noisy instruments at the best of times, but you may not know that elf trumpets are ten times as loud as ordinary human ones. The reason for this is that elf trumpets are made of a strange elf metal called noisium. Noisium is of no use whatever except for making instruments. For hundreds of years, elves thought that noisium was just a useless grey metal sometimes found in rivers. They tried making saucepans out of it, but they melted on the fire. It was just as useless for making money. Coins would stick together in elves' pockets. Knives and forks made of noisium made food taste absolutely horrible. Garden forks and spades made of it seemed to frighten away worms and the kinds of little insects that are good to have in a garden. So everyone was agreed that the best thing to do with noisium was to leave it alone.

It was the great inventor Cabbage Leaf who first realised that noisium might be made into musical instruments. He had a lump of it in the corner of his laboratory, which he used to show students that there are still many mysteries in the elfin world. As Cabbage Leaf grew older, he found that it helped if he walked with a stick. During his lectures to his students, he was fond of waving his stick about. In fact, more than one student lost his hat in the process! One fine day, Cabbage Leaf happened to wave his stick in the direction of the lump of noisium ... and he hit it! BONGGGG! A glorious noise echoed around the laboratory. Cabbage Leaf hit the noisium again ... twice. BINGGGG BONGGGG! went the metal, filling every corner of the room with its rich, ringing sound. And all the glass jars on the laboratory shelves tinkled and jingled too.

Soon after Cabbage Leaf had published his important article on the uses of noisium, every instrument-maker in Elfland was using it to make things that could be banged and blown and twanged and jingled. Before long, no ordinary instruments were made at all. They sounded so thin and weedy beside the ringing tones of the noisium instruments.

Now there are times when you want music to be really loud, but there are probably more times when you don't. When young Twinkletoes began to practise the trumpet, it became clear that he had no idea of the difference between those two kinds of times. He regularly woke up all the babies in Elftown, just when their mothers had rocked them to sleep at last. He made old Acorn's hens stop laying. They felt that the noise made it hard for them to cluck properly, and everyone knows that a chicken who can't cluck can't lay eggs either. Old Mother Sedge, who lived right outside the village, claimed that even in her distant meadows the bees stopped making honey when the trumpet was playing.

Before long, Twinkletoes' playing was the only subject of conversation all over Elftown.

Now Twinkletoes was not an unkind elf, and if he had known about the fuss, he would probably have tried to find somewhere to practise where he couldn't be heard, but he simply didn't know what trouble he had caused. As is often the case, other elves were happier to talk about him behind his back than to stroll up to him in a straightforward way and say, "Now, look here, Twinkletoes old chap, about this trumpet playing..."

To be fair, not everyone complained about Twinkletoes, and that is why the trouble got a lot worse. Some people actually *liked* his trumpeting. Farmer Fern found that his cows gave more milk when Twinkletoes played. The dogs in Elftown *loved* the music and howled with pleasure every time they heard it. Cowslip even said that she thought it cleaned her windows by shaking all the dirt off them!

Very soon, the whole of Elftown had taken up a position on one side or the other. Half of them wanted Twinkletoes' trumpet banned from the whole of Elfland. The other half insisted that Twinkletoes must be allowed to play every day and as often as he liked, especially as he obviously *needed* the practice! For even those who liked Twinkletoes' music agreed that his technique could certainly be improved.

At first, the disagreements were quite friendly, but gradually feelings became stronger. Acorn refused to visit Cowslip because she was on the other side of the argument. Old Mother Sedge wouldn't deliver honey to Petal's new restaurant because she had heard that Petal rather liked being woken by a rousing chorus of "Arise, Elflings All!" every morning. Everywhere you looked, there were scowling faces and cross looks.

For a long time, Twinkletoes was completely unaware of the trouble. He was so interested in his new hobby that he hardly had time to walk down the High Street and see what was going on. It was quite a few weeks before he found that he didn't have another drop of noisium polish in the house and needed to go shopping.

Then what a change he saw! Instead of the merry, laughing greetings he was used to receiving, he found that half his friends crossed the street to avoid him. The other half were almost embarrassingly friendly, clapping him on the back and greeting him as though he had just travelled to the North Pole and back.

It was Cowslip who explained to Twinkletoes what was wrong.

"It's silly really," she said.

"You mean all this is happening because of my trumpet-playing?" asked Twinkletoes. "I simply can't believe it. I had no idea at all."

"Yes," said Cowslip, "but the question is, what are we going to do about it?"

Twinkletoes thought for a moment, scratching his chin.

"Sound-proofing?" he asked.

"Much too expensive," said Cowslip firmly.

"I suppose I could give up my trumpet?" Twinkletoes suggested sadly, shuffling his feet.

"That would only please half the elves in Elftown," said Cowslip. "No, we must think of a better idea somehow."

As Cowslip went on her way later that day, she saw Old Mother Sedge coming towards her. Now Cowslip and Mother Sedge were on opposite sides of the argument but they were great friends. In fact, Mother Sedge had been heard to say that Cowslip was the only sensible elf in Elftown apart from herself. As Cowslip came nearer to her old friend, she heard that she was singing to herself.

Cowslip hesitated. Old Mother Sedge paused and looked up. Then they both smiled.

"We can't go on like this," said Cowslip. "You like music, Mother Sedge, I'm sure, for I heard you singing just now. Couldn't Twinkletoes practise for just a little while each day?"

"You know," said Mother Sedge, "you have given me an idea, my friend. I certainly was singing just now. I find that a rousing chorus every now and then blows the cobwebs away and makes me feel happy on the darkest day, although

I'm always a little afraid other elves will think I'm becoming eccentric in my old age. But shouldn't we all be able to make a noise sometimes, if we feel like it?"

"I was thinking exactly the same thing," agreed Cowslip. "There are times when I feel a lot better if I go into the garden and have a quick scream. But I don't do it very often for fear that people will think Mayflower is trying to murder me!"

"I wonder," said Old Mother Sedge, "are you thinking what I'm thinking, my dear?"

And that is why, if you are thinking of visiting Elftown, I would advise you not to go between half past eight and half past nine in the morning. That is when all the noisiest things you can imagine take place. Acorn shouts at his hens. Cowslip has a good scream. Old Mother Sedge sings her heart out. Some elves vacuum their carpets, while others do all the noisy drilling and hammering that would annoy their neighbours at any other time.

And, of course, Twinkletoes practises his trumpet. I believe he's getting quite good now. It's a pity that no one else can hear him for all the noise that *they* are making, isn't it?

A Name
For an Elf

Cowslip's baby was born in the spring. Mayflower was the proudest elfin father you have ever seen. He ran down the main street of Elftown shouting the good news to everyone he met.

"We've got a little girl!" he called to Twinkletoes, who was admiring his new hat in a shop window and almost jumped out of his skin.

"That's wonderful!" called Twinkletoes, when he had recovered. "What's her name?"

But Mayflower was already halfway down the street.

"It's a girl!" he called to Old Mother Sedge, who had come

into town to buy some labels for her jars of honey.

"What is?" called Mother Sedge, who didn't really keep up with Elftown news.

"Our baby!" shouted Mayflower, rushing past. "She was born at half past nine this morning!"

Now shouting when you're running is almost as bad as shouting with your mouth full. Poor Old Mother Sedge couldn't work out what Mayflower was talking about. Something about a fine morning, wasn't it?

"Yes, it is!" shouted the old lady, which would have confused Mayflower if he wasn't already so

excited and confused that he
hardly noticed.

Acorn was coming out of the
bakery and was almost knocked
to his feet by the rushing elf. Was
there a fire? There was certainly
an emergency of some kind. He
had never seen Mayflower move
so fast. Then he remembered that
Cowslip's baby was due any day.

"Can I help?" he called. "Shall I
fetch the doctor from Goblinville?
What's happening?"

He would probably have been
no wiser than Old Mother Sedge,
if Mayflower hadn't at that
moment turned his head and run
straight into a lamp-post.

Boing! The delighted elf saw a whole constellation of stars spinning around his head and sat down with a bump on the pavement. For a moment, he completely forgot why he was running or anything that had happened that day.

Acorn came trotting up as fast as his creaky joints would let him. The young elf was clearly concussed and needed medical attention at once.

"Now I *am* calling the doctor!" said Acorn, but Mayflower shook his head slowly.

"He's not there," he said in a dreamy voice.

"Not where?" asked Acorn.

"Not in Goblinville," replied Mayflower, watching a particularly pretty shooting star circle the lamp-post and do a double back-flip over his head.

"How do you know?" the old elf wondered. He was becoming a little confused himself now.

"Because I went to Goblinville this morning," said Mayflower, still watching the star, which had begun to dance and wave its hands, which is very odd indeed, for stars, as you probably know, don't usually have hands!

"So where did they say he was?" Acorn persisted. He was more sure than ever now that the young elf needed help.

"He was there," said Mayflower.

"Where?"

"In Goblinville."

"But you silly young elf, you just said…" Acorn began, but at that moment, the mists, the stars and the pain in his forehead suddenly left Mayflower and he was thinking clearly again. (Yes, I know that some elves, and probably Cowslip is one of them, would say that Mayflower *never* thinks clearly, but this was one of the times when he nearly did.)

"I said that the doctor isn't in Goblinville *now*," explained Mayflower. "He *was* there when I called this morning, but right now he's at our house. And," he added, with a great beam across his face, "we've got the most beautiful baby girl you've *ever* seen, and that includes your fourteen granddaughters, Acorn, so there!"

It took a few minutes for this to sink in. Then Acorn shook Mayflower briskly by the hand, offered him many congratulations, mentioned that he'd discuss the business about his *exceptionally* beautiful granddaughters another time, and asked the question that Twinkletoes had asked only a few minutes before.

"What's her name?"

Mayflower slowly stood up and dusted down his jacket. He looked at Acorn with a strangely embarrassed expression and shuffled from foot to foot.

"Well, I don't know," he said, going rather pink.

Acorn looked puzzled. "Is it a secret?" he asked. "If you don't know, who does know?"

"No, no," explained the proud father, "no one knows. That is, we haven't agreed on a name yet."

Now Acorn was an elf of the old school, and to his mind, this was a shocking state of affairs.

"In that case, young elf," he said, "I suggest you stop cavorting up and down the High Street like a demented rabbit and go straight home and *agree* on a name. An elf without a name is like a…"

"Star without hands," finished Mayflower, walking quickly away, which left Acorn wondering whether, after all, he shouldn't look into getting a hearing aid, as his daughter suggested.

Back at home, Mayflower found the doctor preparing to leave, having enjoyed a cup of elf tea with the new mother and given her all sorts of useful advice about looking after the new baby. Cowslip privately thought that she knew a great deal more about looking after babies, having had thirteen brothers herself, than a bachelor goblin doctor, but she was so happy holding her little one that she hardly argued at all.

Mayflower shook the doctor's hand several times and then shook it again to be on the safe side. The doctor looked at him a little sharply and asked if he would like him to look at the large lump that was forming on his forehead, which made Cowslip sigh and laugh and ask what Mayflower had been up to *now*!

"I hope, sweetheart," she smiled, "that you are going to be quite sensible now that you're a *father*. After all, our baby will look to you for advice and help."

Mayflower waved the doctor away, explaining that the lampposts in Elftown were peculiarly badly lit (which would hardly have made sense at the best of times, but especially not in the middle of the day), and shook his hand once more, before shutting

the door firmly behind him. Then
he turned to his wife and put on
his most serious expression.

"Now, Cowslip," he said, "this
can't go on. Now that she's here,
we have *got* to decide on a name
for our baby. Should she be
doing that by the way?"

The baby was waving her little
fists in the air and screwing up
her tiny nose.

"She's fine," said Cowslip, "and
when I'm completely sure that
you've recovered from that
bump on the head, I'll give her to
you to hold. But you are right, my
dear. We really must agree on a
name. Where did I put that book?"

"It's here," said Mayflower, pulling down *The Biggest Ever Elfin Book of Babies' Names* from the shelf. In tiny writing under the title were the words: *including some goblin names that are not too bad.*

Mayflower sat down on a chair and opened the book. "Shall I start at A?" he asked.

"No," replied Cowslip, "we've already been through those. Let's try just letting the book fall open and pointing a finger and seeing what we get."

So Mayflower let the book fall open and pointed his finger and found that it had landed on the number 146. "I don't think we can call her that," he said dubiously, looking at Cowslip and his sleeping daughter.

"Don't be silly," replied his wife. "That's the page number. Be a bit more careful where you point."

So Mayflower tried again and again, and this is how the conversation went:

"Nettle?"

"Name our daughter after a plant that stings? I should think not, Mayflower. Try again."

"Poppy?"

"I had an Aunt Poppy. She had huge feet. We can't have that."

"Pennyroyal?"

"That's a goblin name. No!"

"Mayflower? Oh, how funny, fancy my finger landing on that!"

"I think one Mayflower in this family is quite enough!"

"Nasturtium?"

"Umm, I quite like that."

"I don't. Children at elf school will nickname her 'Nasty'."

"Perhaps you're right."

"Primrose?"

"No."

"Why not? It's a pretty name."

"Yes, and half the little elves at school are called it. I'd like a special name for *our* daughter."

"All right, what about Angelica?"

"Too long."

"It's not as long as Mayflower!"

"And how old were you when you learned to write your name?"

"All right. What about Cowpat?"

"WHAT?"

"Just joking. Snowflake? Rainbow? River? Blossom?"

And so it went on. There never was a name that both Cowslip and Mayflower liked. By evening, the new baby still didn't have a name.

"We'll try again tomorrow," said Cowslip. "We can call her 'Baby' for just one night."

Next morning, Mayflower looked down at his sleeping daughter. She had the most perfect silky eyelashes and the cutest little ears he had ever seen. They made him have a funny feeling from the tips of his toes to the top of his head. He felt that everything was strange and wonderful.

"You know, I don't feel like myself at all," he told Cowslip, as he cuddled the sleeping baby. "It must be because I'm a father now."

"It might be because you bumped your head," said Cowslip.

And strangely enough, as he looked at the baby's perfect face, that gave Mayflower an idea.

"You know," he said, "I once read a book about some people who named their babies after something they saw soon after they were born. Something that made a big impression on them, like a Red Cloud or a Sitting Bull."

Cowslip looked up sharply. "It's a good idea," she said, "but I can tell you now, Mayflower, that there is no way on this beautiful earth that I am going to call my precious little girl … Lamp-post."

"No, no, no," laughed her husband. "A lamp-post wasn't the only thing that made an impression on me yesterday. As I was sitting on the pavement (now don't laugh) I saw, well, sort of saw, inside my head, but as if they were outside in a way…"

"Get on with it!" cried Cowslip.

"Stars!"

"Stars?"

"Yes. But one Star would do."

Cowslip looked at the baby. "Our little Star," she said. "That's beautiful. Hello, little Star."

At that moment, the baby opened her eyes and waved her little hands. Mayflower smiled.

"Stars *do* have hands," he whispered, so that only the most perfect little ears in the world could hear.

Where's
My Hat?

You may remember that Acorn is an elf who is not as young as he used to be. Of course, none of us are as young as we used to be, are we? Even Cowslip's little daughter is older today than she was yesterday. But that is not the point of this story...

The fact is that Acorn is getting rather forgetful. The other day, he put his dinner in the oven and went out to dig in his vegetable patch. He so enjoyed being out in the sunshine that he completely forgot about his dinner. When his rumbling tummy finally reminded him, he ran into the kitchen.

Well, you can imagine, can't you? The dinner was so black and burnt that it was impossible to tell whether it had started off as vegetable stew or beef and carrots. In fact, even Acorn's hens, who are known to eat pretty well anything that is put in front of them, refused to have anything to do with the horrible burnt mess.

Luckily, Acorn had a tin of elf beans in the cupboard, so he did not go hungry, but the next day, the very same thing happened again! Acorn decided that he would take his kitchen timer out into the garden with him. When it rang, after half an hour, he would know that his dinner was ready and go inside to rescue it!

The first time he did this, it worked very well. After half an hour, the timer rang. Acorn fished it out of his jacket pocket and went inside, where he enjoyed a beautifully cooked dinner of cabbage casserole and rice pudding.

Next day was warm and sunny. Acorn didn't need to wear his jacket in the garden. When he had put his dinner in the oven, he picked up the timer and took it outside with him. As he weeded his carrot patch, he put the timer down by his side.

Acorn felt very pleased with his work that morning. When the timer rang, he had cleared a large patch of ground. He put out his hand to pick up the timer ... and it wasn't there!

Where on earth was that timer? *Drrriiiing!* It kept ringing in a really annoying manner, but it was nowhere to be seen.

Poor old Acorn spent fifteen minutes on his hands and knees, working his way back across the rows of carrots until at last he found the timer … right under a pile of weeds. No prizes at all for guessing the state of his dinner when he went inside, but he was so cross that he ate it anyway.

Acorn is not an elf to give up easily, however. That night, he tied a piece of string to the timer. Next morning, he tied the string around his arm and wore the timer like an enormous watch. It looked ridiculous, but it worked.

Over the following months, Acorn came up with quite a few good ideas to stop himself forgetting important things. He tried tying knots in his handkerchief, but there were soon so many knots that it hurt his nose to blow it! After that, he carried a little notebook with him everywhere he went, in which he made a list of all the things he really must not forget. That worked really well except on the days when he forgot the notebook! Even Acorn had to laugh when that happened.

As a matter of fact, Acorn was not really so forgetful as he thought he was. It was just that he spent so much time trying not to forget things, he had very little time to be sure to remember them! He would sit for hours making list after list, when he could have been doing things so that they didn't have to go on a list in the first place.

Mayflower and Twinkletoes had a talk about it one afternoon. They were both worried that their old friend was making himself worried and unhappy for no reason at all. But they really couldn't think of a way to persuade him to relax and enjoy his life as he used to do.

As things turned out, Acorn solved the problem himself, quite by accident.

One chilly morning, Acorn was getting ready to go out and do some shopping. He put on his overcoat, his scarf and his gloves. Then he stretched out his hand for his hat. It wasn't there!

Acorn checked under the other clothes on his coat rack. There was no hat. Then he got down on his hands and knees and searched on the floor, in case it had fallen off. There was no hat to be seen anywhere.

"This is ridiculous," said Acorn to himself. "I was wearing it only yesterday. Now where can I have put it? I really am getting to be a very forgetful old elf."

Acorn searched upstairs in the bedroom. He looked in the kitchen. He even checked in the oven in case he had put his hat in there by mistake!

After half an hour, Acorn was becoming desperate. Where on earth was that hat? He began to look in places that he knew perfectly well he had not been near for weeks. When he found himself searching in a box in the attic, which to his certain knowledge had not been opened since his old Aunt Anemone was a girl, Acorn knew that he was being a silly old elf and must stop searching.

"I'll just have to go out without my hat," he said. "It's not the end of the world, after all."

So Acorn set off down the road, clutching one of his famous lists so that he didn't forget what he needed for his supper that day.

When he reached the green-grocer's, Acorn peered down at his list.

"I'll have two pairs of socks and a pair of underpants, please," he said firmly.

Of course, the shopkeeper couldn't help laughing. "That's your laundry list!" he chuckled.

Acorn looked embarrassed. "I'm so forgetful now, I can't even remember the right list," he said. "And I couldn't find my hat at all this morning."

The greengrocer gave Acorn a strange look. "My friend," he said, " you are trying too hard. Forget your lists and you will find that you remember much more … like your hat, for instance!"

Acorn knew the shopkeeper was right. His worries seemed to fly away, as he put up his hand and found his hat … on his own head!

The Secret Recipe

Everyone in Elftown agreed that Petal's restaurant was a great success, and one of the reasons was her extra special blueberry cake. Any elf who was feeling a little tired in the middle of the morning or around teatime simply hurried into the restaurant for a slice of cake. In two minutes he felt better … and ready for another slice!

Many elves asked Petal for the recipe of her special cake, but she would just smile mysteriously and shake her head.

"I was given this recipe by a very wise woman," she said. "I promised her that I would not tell it to anyone else, unless they knew the secret already!"

That didn't seem to make sense at all. Why would anyone need to ask if they already knew the recipe?

Of all the elves who longed to know what Petal put in her blueberry cake, Old Mother Sedge was the most curious.

"I can taste honey," she would say, munching a large slice.

"Yes," said Petal. "It is honey from your own bees, Mother Sedge. Isn't it delicious?"

"And there are blueberries in here," cried Mother Sedge triumphantly, taking another bite.

"Well, there would be, wouldn't there, in a blueberry cake?" smiled Petal. "Another slice?"

By the end of the week, and several more slices of blueberry cake, Old Mother Sedge had guessed all the ingredients except one. Yes, there was flour and butter and eggs. There were lots of blueberries and at least five dripping spoonfuls of honey. But what was the last ingredient?

"Nuts?" asked the old lady.

"What kind of nuts?" asked Petal in return.

"Hazelnuts? Brazil nuts? Peanuts? Pecans? Walnuts? Almonds? Cashews?" Mother

Sedge was thinking so hard that her face was as wrinkled as a walnut itself.

"No," said Petal. "There are no nuts in the cake at all."

"Fruit?" asked Mother Sedge. "Apart from the blueberries?"

"What kind of fruit?" asked Petal, with a mischievous smile.

"Er ... apples? Plums? Peaches? Blackberries? Raspberries? Pears? Strawberries? Apricots? Mangoes? Bananas? Nectarines? Pineapples? Prunes? Grapefruit? Oranges? Lemons? Blackcurrants? Redcurrants? White currants? Gooseberries?" Old Mother Sedge stopped to catch her breath.

"No," laughed Petal. "I can tell you that blueberries are the only kind of fruit in my special cake."

Poor Mother Sedge! The more she asked, the less she knew.

Then, one morning, the old lady happened to visit Acorn when he was making an apple pudding for his supper.

"At least I know what goes into one of *those*," she sighed, and she repeated all the ingredients one by one.

"That's right," said Acorn, "but for a really fine apple pudding, you've missed one out, or at least, that's what my dear old mother used to say, bless her soul."

"Not you too!" cried Old Mother Sedge. "There are more secret ingredients in Elftown than I've had hot dinners!"

"Not at all, my dear," said Acorn. "The secret ingredient is the same in all my cooking, and I must say it makes a difference. I'm quite sure that you know it as well as I do, but if you like, I'll whisper it in your ear."

So Acorn bent down and whispered the secret ingredient, and Old Mother Sedge went quite pink for a moment, before she smiled at her old friend.

"You're quite right, of course," she said. "My mother used to say the same, and I've never tasted anything to beat her raspberry tarts … except perhaps Petal's blueberry cake."

Next time Old Mother Sedge sat down to a slice of Petal's special creation, she smiled at the younger elf but asked no questions.

"I can see that you have guessed the secret," laughed Petal. "The wise woman who told it to me was my mother. She said, 'Everything you make will taste better if you put in a little spoonful of love.' That's the secret ingredient in all my cooking."

She was quite right, you know. You should try it sometime.

Goodnight, Little Goblin

There was once a little goblin called Bramble. He was a very good little goblin in *almost* every way. He played nicely with his little sister, even when she sat on his racing car and squashed it. He ate up all his dinner, even when it was rice pudding. He even helped his mother with the washing up … sometimes. But there was one thing that Bramble would not do. He would not go to bed when his mother told him it was time.

Bramble's parents had tried everything to persuade their son to go to bed. They had tried threatening him with rice

pudding for a week. They had
tried rewarding him with no rice
pudding for two weeks. They had
even decorated his bedroom
with cars and aeroplanes, so that
Bramble couldn't wait to go into
his bedroom at night.

But being in his bedroom
didn't mean that Bramble was in
his bed, and it certainly didn't
mean that he was asleep. There
never was a goblin boy with so
many excuses for staying awake.

"Why aren't you asleep,
Bramble?" his mother would ask,
peeping around the door.

"It's much too light in here,"
Bramble would reply. "The stars

are shining right into my room. Look! No one could sleep in all this starlight."

"I see," said his mother, and she went downstairs. The next day, Bramble's mother made him extra-thick curtains, so that not one drop of starlight shone into his room. But the next night, when she peeped round the door, Bramble was wide awake as usual.

"What is it now, Bramble?" she asked wearily.

"I'm too hot," said Bramble, "with those thick curtains over the window, and anyway, I can't see to play now."

"You're not supposed to be playing!" cried his mother. "It's night time, Bramble, when all little goblins should be in bed and fast asleep. Don't let me find you awake again."

But Bramble just did not want to sleep. There were too many interesting things to do to waste time sleeping.

When Bramble's parents were at their wits' ends, his Great Uncle Gorse came to stay. Great Uncle Gorse was a rather stern old goblin. His great niece and great nephew were a little bit afraid of him, because they had once overheard their mother saying that the old man knew quite a lot about magic. Now, when he peered at them over his spectacles, he looked too ordinary to be able to do magic.

Bramble rather thought that magic was a made-up thing in any case. "I think it only happened in olden times and in stories," he told his sister. "There isn't any magic around today."

But that was where Bramble was quite, quite wrong. Great Uncle Gorse certainly did know some magic. In fact, he knew more than almost any other living goblin.

It was not long before Great Uncle Gorse found out about Bramble's unwillingness to sleep.

"That's ridiculous," he told Bramble's mother. "What have you tried?"

"Everything," she sighed.

"Have you tried … a little … well, of the *old* ways, my dear?"

"You mean m-m-m-magic?" gasped his niece. "Oh, I don't think that would be a good idea. Bramble is very young, you know, and magic is such dangerous stuff."

"I promise you that no harm will come to the boy," said the old goblin. "Now, this is what I suggest..."

The next night, Bramble went to bed as usual. But did he go to sleep? Oh no! First he got out of bed and played with his cars for a while. (His mother came in twice to plead with him to go to sleep during this time.) Then he pretended to be a spaceman and jumped across his bed as though he was on the moon. (His mother came in once more while this was going on.) Being a spaceman made Bramble think about explorers, so he began an expedition to find out what was under his bed. (His mother came in again while he was doing this and was nearly frightened out of her wits when she couldn't see Bramble *anywhere*.)

By the time Bramble had finished his under-bed exploration, and found several toys that he had completely forgotten about, the whole house was quiet. His mother and father and Great Uncle Gorse had all gone to bed.

Bramble made himself a sandwich and read an interesting book about pirates, using his torch under the bedclothes.

After that, even Bramble was beginning to feel rather sleepy. Perhaps it was time for a quick snooze after all. But Bramble quickly found a very strange thing. He couldn't close his eyes!

"How horrible!" you will say. "The poor boy's eyeballs will shrivel up!" Perhaps I have given the wrong impression. It wasn't actually that Bramble couldn't close his eyes. He simply couldn't *keep* them closed. He could blink, but when he tried to keep his eyes shut, they just bounced open again.

At first, Bramble wasn't too worried, but the longer this

happened, the more he found
that the one thing he really
wanted to do was to go to sleep.
He tried everything he could
think of, but the fact of the
matter is that it is very difficult
indeed to go to sleep with your
eyes open.

Before long, Bramble saw the
pink light of dawn creeping
through his window. Morning
was coming, and he hadn't had a
single wink of sleep.

There were lots of interesting
things happening that day, but
Bramble didn't really feel like
any of them. He played in the
goblin goal in an elves *v.* goblins

football match and let in twelve goals. He did an experiment in his science lesson and nearly set fire to the classroom. When it was time to go home, he was almost run over by a goblin cart because he was too tired to concentrate when he crossed the road outside the school. It really was one of the most dreadful days he had ever known.

That evening at supper, Bramble could hardly keep his eyes open, although, of course, he couldn't keep them shut, either. Each time he looked up, he could see Great Uncle Gorse peering at him through his spectacles with a strange expression on his face.

"What would you like to do now more than anything else in the world?" the old goblin asked his great nephew.

"Oh, Great Uncle Gorse," cried Bramble, "I just want to go to bed!"

One smile from Great Uncle Gorse lifted the spell, and Bramble was asleep before his head hit the pillow.

I have heard that he now goes to sleep as well as any little boy in Goblinville. And if he ever goes back to his old ways, Great Uncle Gorse has an open invitation to come to stay…

Titles in this Series include